Cecil and Alice rode their bikes to the school fair.

"Let's sit in those seats in the center of that bench near the fence," said Cecil.

Cecil and Alice took
seats on the bench.
They watched their pal
Cedric in a race. "He is
fast!" said Alice.

After the race, they
went to a booth where
Mrs. Pace was painting
faces. Alice got a flower
painted on her cheek.

Cecil had his face painted with stars. "Let's go to the bean-toss booth next," said Alice.

Mr. Clancy ran the
bean-toss booth.
"Will you play?" he asked
Alice and Cecil.
"Yes," said Alice. She
gave Mr. Clancy ten cents.

6

Alice tossed her first
bag without luck. But
her next bag fell inside
the square!

Alice got to pick a
prize. She chose a
red pencil.

"Alice," Cecil said, "I
am hungry now. I will
get something to eat.
Please wait on the
bench and save
my place."

Cecil waited in line at the food stand. "This is a slow line," Cecil said to himself.

Alice waited and
waited for Cecil. "I am
hungry now, too," Alice
said to herself. "I will
get something to eat."

Alice came back with a hot dog and celery sticks. Cecil was back on the bench. His plate was empty.

"Where is your lunch?"
asked Alice.
Cecil stuck out his
tummy. "In here,"
he said.

"Guess what I had?"
said Cecil, with a
smile. The braces on
his teeth glittered in
the sun.

"I see cheese stuck in
your braces and red
stuff on your plate. I
bet you had a slice of
pizza," Alice said.

"That is a good guess!"
said Cecil.